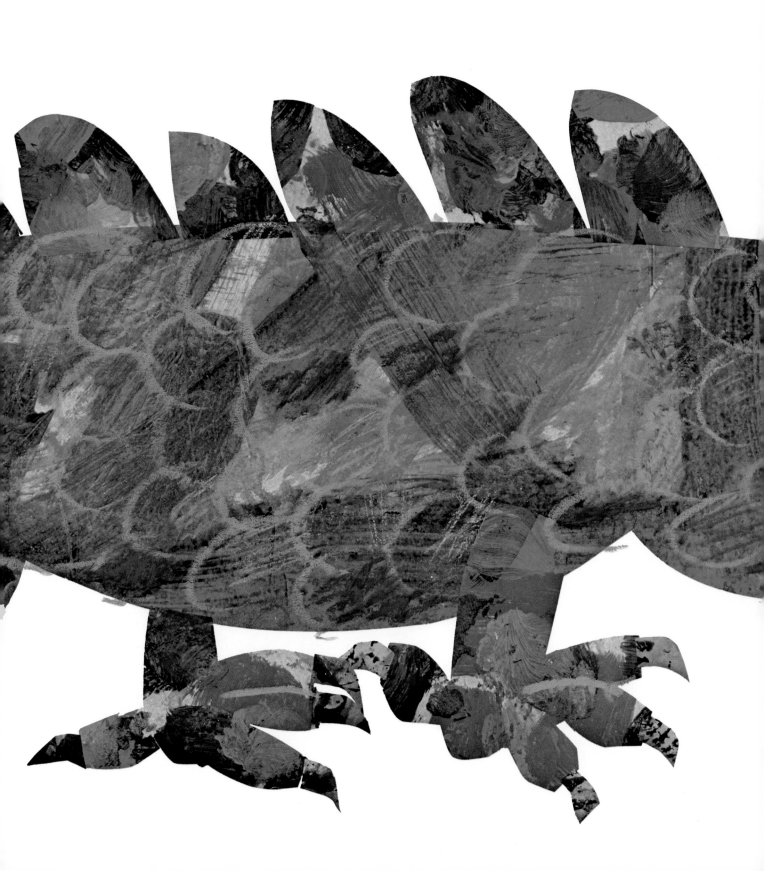

ERIC CARLE'S TREASURY OF CLASSIC STORIES FOR CHILDREN

by Aesop, Hans Christian Andersen and the Brothers Grimm
selected, retold and illustrated by Eric Carle

SCHOLASTIC INC.
New York   Toronto   London   Auckland   Sydney

FOR NADJA AND TERESA

Portions of this book appeared in *Twelve Tales from Aesop*, retold and illustrated by Eric Carle,
published in 1980 by Philomel Books, New York; *Seven Stories by Hans Christian Andersen*
published in 1978 by Franklin Watts, New York; and in *Eric Carle's Storybook: Seven Tales by the
Brothers Grimm* published in 1976 by Franklin Watts, New York. Grateful acknowledgement is
given for permission to use these materials in the current volume.

ISBN 0-590-50213-1

12 11 10 9 8 7 6   8 9/9 0/0

Printed in the U.S.A.   14

CONTENTS

TOM THUMB

A poor woodcutter sat by the fire one evening, while his wife sat across from him, spinning. He said, "What a sad thing it is that we have no children. We live too quietly. A child would cheer us up."

"Yes," said his wife. "I'd even be glad of one the size of my thumb."

Some time later they had a son, and sure enough, he was no bigger than a thumb. They named him Tom Thumb, and they loved him dearly and gave him the best of care.

Time passed. Tom never grew any larger, but he was strong and healthy. He became a quick, bright child who did well at whatever he tried.

One morning, when his father was getting ready to go into the forest to cut some wood, he said, "I wish I had someone to bring me the horse and cart later on."

"Leave the horse to me," said Tom. "I can bring him."

"Very well," replied his father.

That afternoon Tom climbed up and sat between the horse's ears. "Gittup," he called to the horse in a big brave voice, and away they went together.

Two strangers were passing through the wood and saw the horse galloping. They heard Tom calling to it to turn right or left, but there was no one to be seen. "That's very strange," they said. "Let's follow the cart and see what happens when it stops."

Soon the men came to the spot where Tom's father was waiting, and they hid behind a tree. "Here I am, Father," Tom called. "Didn't I drive the horse well?"

"Yes, you're a fine boy," said the woodcutter, as he lifted Tom to his shoulder.

"We could make a fortune with that odd little fellow," said one of the men. "If we showed him in the towns for money, people would pay to see him. Let's buy him."

"Hey, there," he said to the woodcutter. "Here's a fine piece of gold. Sell us the boy. We'll take good care of him."

"No," said the woodcutter. "He is all my wife and I have, and we love him with all our hearts."

But Tom whispered in his father's ear, "Take the gold and don't worry about me. I'll be home before you know it."

"Well, all right then," said the woodcutter, and he took the gold.

One of the men put Tom on the rim of his hat and they all said their good-byes. Tom's father went one way with the horse and the wood and the piece of gold. The two men went the other way with Tom riding on the hat.

After a while, Tom called, "Let me down."

"No," said the men. "You'll just run away."

"But it's important business," said Tom.

So the men put Tom down in the grass. Quick as a wink he ran into a mouse hole. "Good-bye, gentlemen," he called.

The men looked everywhere, but they could not see Tom. They poked in the hole, but he stayed safely out of reach. "We've been tricked," they said angrily, and they went on their way.

When Tom came out of the hole, the moon was up. "Traveling at night is risky," Tom said. So he curled up in a snail shell that lay in the field nearby.

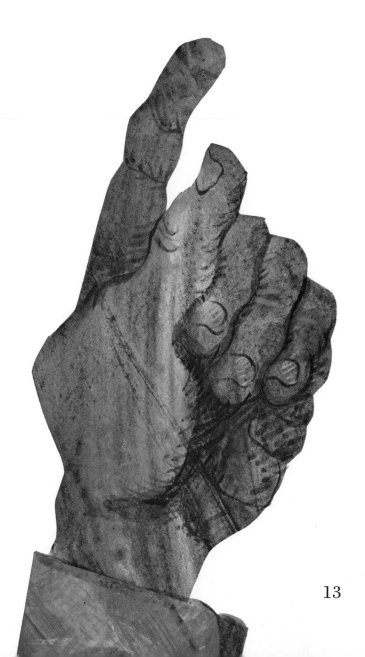

Just as he was falling asleep, he heard two men passing by.

"That rich man has gold and silver and jewels, but how can we get in to steal them?" asked one man.

"I can help you," shouted Tom.

"Whose voice is that? Where are you?" asked the thieves.

"Here. In the grass."

When the thieves saw Tom, they laughed.

"How could a little fellow like you help us?" they said.

"I could slip into the house and hand out to you whatever you want," said Tom.

"All right, it's worth a try," said the thieves. "Come along."

But when Tom got inside the house, he called out in a loud voice, "What do you want? Shall I hand out everything?"

"S-sh," said the thieves. "Not so loud."

Tom pretended not to understand.

"Hold out your hands," he shouted. "Here's some gold."

The maid heard the noise and came with a lamp. Quickly the thieves ran away, and Tom, pleased with himself, tiptoed out to the barn. There he went to sleep in a pile of soft hay, thinking he'd be home in time for dinner the next day. In the morning the maid came to feed the cow. She picked up the pile of hay where Tom was sleeping. When he woke up, he was in the cow's mouth. The cow swallowed, and Tom slid into her stomach. He screamed, but the maid had already left to do the baking.

Later the maid came back to milk the cow. Imagine her surprise when she heard a voice inside it, crying, "Let me out. Let me out."

She ran to her master. "The cow is talking," she said.

Her master came to listen. Again a voice called, "Let me out. Let me out."

The master turned pale with fright. "It's an evil spirit," he said. "We must kill the cow."

So he butchered the cow and threw her stomach into the rubbish heap, with Tom still inside. Tom twisted and turned, trying to work his way out of the stomach. Just as he was beginning to sniff fresh air a starving wolf came by. The wolf pounced on the stomach and gulped it down—but still Tom did not lose courage.

"Dear friend," called Tom from inside the wolf, "I know where you can find the most delicious food."

"Where is that?" asked the wolf.

"The woodcutter's house," said Tom. "I'll tell you how to get there."

When they came to the house, Tom said, "Go to the narrow window in the back, and force yourself through. That's where the pantry is."

The wolf pushed his way through the narrow window and ate until he was stuffed full. But when he tried to leave, his stomach had grown so big and fat he could not get out.

Now Tom began to scream as loud as he could, "Help, help!"

"Be quiet," said the wolf. "You'll wake everyone up." But Tom kept on screaming.

Before long, the woodcutter and his wife heard the noise and came with an ax. Upon seeing the wolf, the woodcutter shouted, "I'll get you, you thief!" And he swung the ax back for the kill.

"Father, Father!" yelled Tom. "I'm in the wolf's belly."

"Don't worry, I won't hurt you," the woodcutter replied, and he struck the wolf dead with one blow on its head. Then he cut the wolf open and took Tom out. "Thank heaven you're back," he said. "Where on earth have you been?"

"I've been seeing the world," said Tom. "Now I am happy to breathe the fresh air again. I've been inside a mouse hole, a snail shell, a cow's stomach, and a wolf's belly. And now I'll stay right here with you."

"And we will never give you away again for all the gold in the world," said his parents, as they hugged and kissed their child.

THE FISHERMAN AND HIS WIFE

There was once a poor fisherman who lived with his wife in a tiny hut by the sea. Each morning he went down to the shore and cast his net for fish. One day he pulled up a fish with gold and silver scales. "Oh," said the fish, "I beg you to let me go. I am really an enchanted prince, and not at all good to eat."

"Prince or no prince, any fish who can talk has earned its freedom," said the fisherman, and he let the fish go.

When he told his wife what had happened, she said, "You nincompoop, that was a magic fish, the kind that makes wishes come true. You should have made a wish."

"But we have everything we need," said the fisherman.

His wife did not listen. "Tomorrow," she said, "catch the fish again and ask it for a big house like those in the city. And I'd like a black dress with white frills, too."

The fisherman did not like to oppose his wife so he cast his net in

the same place the next day. Little waves were beating against the shore. Soon he pulled up the fish. "What is it?" asked the fish with the silver and gold scales.

"My wife says I should have made a wish," said the fisherman. "She wants a big house like those in the city, and a black dress with white frills."

"Go home," said the fish. "She has them already."

The fisherman went home. Sure enough, his wife, in a black dress with white frills, stood in front of a big house.

A week passed, and the fisherman's wife began to find the house too small. "Find the magic fish," she said. "I want to be a queen and live in a castle."

"But surely now we have everything we need," said the fisherman.

"I must be queen," his wife kept saying. Finally the fisherman gave in and went to the water.

The water along the shore was black, and the wind was high. The fisherman said to the fish when it appeared, "My wife wants to be queen and live in a castle."

"Go home," said the fish. "She already has her wish."

The fisherman went home and, indeed, his wife was now a queen. She stood at the door of a splendid big castle.

"Ah," said the fisherman. "Now you are queen. There is nothing more you can want."

"I am not satisfied with being queen," said his wife. "Go to the fish and tell it I want to be pope."

"Oh, no," said the fisherman. "This time you are asking too much. I do not want to go."

But in the end he went to find the fish. The waves were as high as mountains, and the sky was black. In fright, the fisherman said, "My wife now wants to be pope."

"Go home," said the fish. "She has her wish."

The fisherman went home and found a great church decorated in gold. Tall candles burned before his wife, who was dressed in a pope's robes.

"Now surely you cannot wish for anything more," he said.

"I will think about it," replied his wife. That night she could not sleep, thinking of what else she might be. She got up early, just as the sun was rising. "Ah," she thought, "I should like to be the one who makes the sun rise."

She awoke her husband. "Go to the fish," she commanded. "Tell it I want to make the sun rise. I want to be ruler of the universe."

In terror, the fisherman went to the shore. A wild storm was raging. "Oh, fish," shouted the fisherman above the noise of the wind, "my wife wants to be ruler of the universe."

"Go home," said the fish. And the fisherman went home. He found his wife dressed in her old clothes inside their little hut.

For the rest of their lives the fisherman and his wife lived in the little hut by the sea. Every day the fisherman went to the shore and cast his net. As the years went by, he pulled up hundreds of fish, but never again did he see the magic gold- and silver-scaled fish who could talk and grant wishes.

THE MAGIC BOOTS

A well-known judge loved to talk about the good old times.

Whether he was visiting someone else or someone was visiting him, it wasn't long before he began talking about the olden days and how much better they had been:

"The people used to be more honest."

"The sausages used to be bigger."

"The weather used to be warmer."

"It used to be better when we had a king."

And so forth, and so forth.

And in the end he would say with a sigh, "Ah, and they used to have fairy queens, but not anymore."

Now, that seemed to be true. Not much was heard about fairy queens anymore. Where had they all gone? Had they lived only once upon a time? Well, we shall see.

One day a fairy queen came to the judge's house. Of course, he did not recognize her as a fairy. She looked like an ordinary person. She sold boots and galoshes.

"In the olden days they used to make better boots," said the judge.

But he bought a pair, as he needed them badly. They were magic boots, but the judge did not know it. They could make one's wishes come true.

In the evening the judge drank a glass of wine and then went for a walk. It was a habit of his: a glass of wine, a walk, and then bedtime. He put on his coat and hat and his new boots, or rather his *magic* boots, and stepped outside his home on 8 Maple Street.

He locked the front door, saying to himself, "In the good old days it was not necessary to lock one's door.

"Ah, the good old days," hummed the judge. "I wish they were here again." And with that, he fell into a big puddle. As he sat up, he noticed that there was mud and dirt all over the street.

"What's this?" cried the judge. "Don't they clean the streets anymore?" Of course, he did not know that the magic boots had taken him back into the past, into the olden days.

He could hardly see as he struggled to get up. The streetlights, it seemed, had all gone out. Only a dim candle several houses away cast a faint light on the street.

"I'll complain to the Public Health Department about this," thought the judge. Just then, someone threw rubbish out of a window. It hit the poor judge on his head, and he fell down again. A man and a woman dressed very strangely helped him get up. They spoke to him, but their words sounded so odd that the judge hardly knew what they were saying. At last he understood that they were telling him to walk more in the middle of the road. There the rubbish would not hit him so easily.

"They must have been to a fancy dress party and must be drunk," thought the judge, because the man and woman talked so strangely and looked so unusual. "Or am I dreaming?" Shaking his head in confusion, the judge decided to go home. "But where am I?" he asked himself. His house seemed to have disappeared, and he did not recognize the street at all.

The judge went on walking along the dark road. At last he came to a river. Two men were sitting on the bank.

"Where is the bridge?" asked the judge.

"What bridge do ye mean, noble sir? Have ye need of a ferry boat? The cost is only one gulden," said the two men.

"What are you talking about?" asked the judge. "Where can I get a taxi?"

"Taxi?" asked the two, looking at each other. One of them put his finger on his forehead as if to say, "He's crazy." At that the judge stormed away into the night.

"I had only one small glass of wine," thought the judge. "I cannot be drunk. Or can I?" He didn't know what to think.

Soon he met another man in an odd costume. "Where can I find a telephone to call a taxi?" asked the judge. But the man just looked at him, not understanding a word.

"There must be a telephone booth somewhere," said the judge to the man. The man scratched his head and ran away.

The judge walked on until finally he heard strange music and singing and glasses clinking against each other. He had come to a tavern. He went inside and looked around. The guests all seemed rough and outlandish. They had brought some goats and chickens with them. The room was thick with smoke and noises and smells.

"Ah, this must be the fancy dress party," thought the judge. He asked for a lemonade.

"A what?" asked the waitress. "My dear sir, what do ye mean? We have ale and mead for comfort."

At that a guest turned toward the judge. "From whence have ye come?" said the stranger.

"I live nearby," answered the judge. "Right near the railway station."

"The rail-wa-we-wy? What do ye mean?"

"Well, you go to the traffic light and then you turn—"

By now everybody was looking at the poor judge.

"Traffic light?" someone asked. "What is that?"

The judge felt confused. He took off his glasses. Perhaps something was wrong with them. But the nearest guest grabbed them from him and examined them carefully. Then he handed them to the others to look at. They all oohed and aahed. They had never seen glasses before.

"There must be an evil demon in thy head," said a toothless old woman.

"He should be given twenty lashes," said someone else.

Now the judge was frightened. He ran for the door. Out he went, and had almost escaped when two men jumped for his feet, to tackle him. Just in time, the judge managed to wiggle his feet out of his boots. Down the street he raced, leaving the boots behind—and the magic with them.

Now everything seemed changed. The street was brighter and the houses looked familiar.

"Dear me," said the judge. "That wine must have been stronger than I thought."

Just then a taxi drove by.

"Taxi, taxi!" shouted the judge and climbed, in his socks, inside the taxi. "Take me to 8 Maple Street, please."

"Yes, sir," said the driver.

As the taxi with the judge in it drove away, the fairy queen appeared and picked up a pair of boots that stood halfway inside the doorway of a house. "My, my," she giggled, and put the boots into a shopping bag. No one noticed her. After all, she looked quite ordinary.

THE RABBIT AND THE TURTLE

A rabbit and a turtle were looking for something to do to while away the afternoon.

"How about a race?" suggested the rabbit, who was a very fast runner.

"Couldn't we do something else?" asked the turtle, who was not.

"You are just afraid that you are going to lose," said the rabbit.

"I am not," declared the turtle.

So it was decided to have a race. They asked Mr. Fox to be the judge, and off they went.

The rabbit with his long legs sped down the path so fast he seemed to be flying. But the turtle with his short legs and his heavy shell had a hard time moving at all. Soon the rabbit was so far ahead, he decided to sit down for a little rest. After a long, long time the turtle slowly passed by the rabbit.

"What's the matter, giving up?" asked the turtle.

"Don't worry," said the rabbit and waved. "Just go on. I'll soon catch up with you."

The turtle waved back and plodded on huffing and puffing.

It was a beautiful afternoon. The sun was warm, the birds sang in the meadows, butterflies and ladybugs flew through the air. A gentle wind bent the grass and the flowers. Soon the rabbit sank into a deep sleep. When he woke up, the moon and the stars shone in the night sky.

"Well," said the rabbit, "I must catch up with slowpoke turtle."

He brushed himself off and ran after the turtle.

But when the rabbit came around the last bend of the road he saw the fox pinning a winner's medal on the turtle's chest!

"Slow and steady has won many races," said Mr. Fox.

THE CAT AND THE MOUSE

A young mouse, sick and tired of being chased by the cat, had an idea. The mouse called in the whole family and proclaimed, "We mice must protect ourselves from the cat, once and for all!"

"Yes, yes!" cried all the mice.

"We must be able to run around freely any time and anywhere we wish to do so."

"Right, right!" shrieked the other mice.

"I know how to outwit the cat," went on the proud young mouse.

"How?" asked the others.

"With this bell," said the young mouse, pointing to a shiny new bell. "When the cat is asleep we shall fasten the bell around his neck. When he moves, the bell will ring. That way we can hear the cat before the cat sneaks up on us."

"Bravo, bravo!" cried the mice.

The young mouse bowed and smiled.

"Long live our genius!" shouted the mice.

The young mouse took another bow.

"Question," said a weak voice from the back of the room. "Who will put the bell around the cat's neck?"

All the mice turned around to look at their grandmother, who had asked the question. She was an old mouse, wrinkled and stooped.

"A volunteer, of course," answered the young mouse.

"Who will volunteer?" asked the grandmother.

Everybody looked at everybody else. No one volunteered. And that is why cats still catch mice, to this very day.

THE MONKEY AND THE FOX

When the wise and beloved old king of the jungle had died, all the animals got together to elect a new ruler. Each animal told the others why he would be the best king. When it was the monkey's turn, he put on the old king's crown and his velvet robe and did a wonderful imitation of the king. He even made a short speech in the old king's voice.

"It's almost like having our dear king back again," said the animals and they promptly elected the monkey to be their new king. Only the fox disagreed. He tried to warn the other animals that they were making a mistake.

"It is not enough just to be able to imitate the old king," said the fox. "The monkey is good at that, but he has no sense at all. He certainly is not wise enough to be your leader."

But the animals did not listen to him.

A few days later the fox noticed a trap in the forest. The people from the zoo had put it up to catch the monkey.

"I have noticed something curious in the jungle," said the fox to the monkey.

"Let's go and look at it," answered the monkey.

Soon they came to a large net with a banana hanging under the middle of it. Without thinking twice, the monkey reached for the banana. As he touched the fruit the net fell over him. The monkey was caught. The people who had hidden behind the trees rushed out, tied up the monkey and took him to their zoo. A little later the fox went to the zoo and visited the monkey.

"You traitor," cried the monkey. "You have betrayed your king."

"You have betrayed yourself," said the fox. "A king who falls for the first trap that has been set for him is not a good king. A king who is so foolish would not serve his animals well."

And that is the truth.

41

THE WILD SWANS

In a distant land there lived a king and his queen. They had twelve children—eleven boys and a girl, Elisa, who was the youngest. They all loved each other very much and had a happy time together.

One day the queen became ill. All the doctors were called in, but they could not help her. She died. And the king and the twelve children and all the people of the land were overcome with great sadness. She had been a good queen. Even the sun mourned and stayed behind the dark clouds longer than anyone could remember.

After a year the people asked their king to marry again, and he found a new queen. She was beautiful—but she was a witch! She wanted the king all to herself and decided to get rid of the children as soon as possible.

Soon after the honeymoon was over, the king announced that he and his companions were going hunting. After the king had left and the children had gone to bed and to sleep, the evil queen went to the boys' bedroom. She spoke some strange, magic words and the boys turned into swans.

"Fly away. Never return," she called after them as eleven wild swans with tiny silver crowns on their heads flew out of the window into the night sky.

When the king returned, he asked to see his children. But, of course, the boys were gone.

"They have decided to go out and see the world," said the evil queen with a smile.

"Strange," said the king. "Why did they not wait for my return?"

"You know how it is with boys," said the evil queen.

Elisa could not believe that her brothers would have left without saying good-bye. She knew something was wrong, but she did not know what. She was now so lonely and sad. She missed her brothers more than anything in the world and cried for them often.

Her stepmother slapped and screamed at her whenever the king was away. But when the king was nearby, the evil queen pretended that she loved her. Elisa grew pale and thin.

"A change of air would be good for Elisa. She is now fifteen years

old," said the evil queen one day. "It is time for her to go and live in another kingdom. There she can learn the ways of other people."

"I agree with that," said the king. "I shall be sad, though." But he wanted a good education for his daughter.

"Dear Father, I shall miss you, too," said Elisa. "Perhaps it will be good for me to go away from here. Without my brothers, it has been so lonesome. And if I'm lucky, I might even find them somewhere."

A handsome carriage, drawn by four white horses, was prepared for Elisa's trip. Elisa kissed her father a sad farewell and climbed in. A driver in a fine uniform snapped the whip, trumpets sounded, and

off they went. From inside the carriage, Elisa waved until she could not see the castle anymore.

But the evil queen was plotting against Elisa. She had told the driver to abandon the girl alone in the deep forest.

When they were far inside the forest, the evil man stopped. He pushed Elisa out of the carriage and quickly drove away. She ran after the carriage. But she couldn't catch up, and soon it was out of sight. The clatter of the galloping horses grew faint and finally stopped. The forest was still and strange.

"Help, help!" cried Elisa. "Help, help!" it echoed back, as if to make fun of her.

45

The shadows grew longer, and it was so dark that Elisa couldn't see her own hand. She dropped to the ground and cried all night. The next day Elisa began to wander under the trees, but as hard as she tried, she could not find her way out. She walked this way and that, but always the forest stretched around her on all sides. She was frightened and she was lonely and she longed for her father and brothers.

The forest plants and animals tried to help her. An apple tree let an apple fall to the ground, and she ate the apple. A squirrel dropped a nut in front of her, and she ate the nut. A blackbird led her to a blueberry bush, and she ate some berries. A deer made a path before her. She came to a stream and she cupped her hands and drank the sweet water. Then she took off her dress and bathed in the cool stream.

When the sun went down and it grew dark, fireflies with their tiny torches showed Elisa the way to a cave. Inside, she found a bed made of the softest green moss. There she fell asleep, but not before she had cried many, many tears.

For days, weeks, months, and finally years the forest became Elisa's prison. The trees, the animals, and the sun were good to her, but she could not find her way out of the deep forest. Every night before she fell asleep on her soft green bed of moss, she cried bitterly. She thought of her brothers every day and she wished that they would come and find her.

Then, one night, a beautiful fairy appeared to Elisa. Was it a dream or was it real? Elisa could not tell.

"Tomorrow, when you wake up, follow the river downstream," the fairy said.

In the morning, Elisa followed the river downstream. She jumped from rock to rock, walked along fallen trees, crawled up and down the embankments. At last, as the sun was almost ready to set, she came to the spot where the river flowed into the ocean. In the sand she saw eleven white feathers. As she bent down to pick them up, she heard a strange sound in the air. She looked up and saw eleven swans with tiny silver crowns on their heads. They circled, then landed near her. Just then the sun disappeared below the horizon, and the swans turned into eleven young men. Elisa had not seen her brothers for over three years, but she recognized them right away.

She shouted with joy and they all kissed and hugged each other. They hardly knew where to begin telling and asking what had happened since they had last been together.

"Our stepmother has cast an evil spell on us," said the youngest of the brothers. "When the sun comes up in the morning, we turn into wild swans, and when the sun sets in the evening we turn into

men. When the sun goes down, we must make sure that we are not in the air or we would fall down and be killed. We live across the ocean. It takes a day and a night and another day for us to get to the other land. In the middle of the ocean, a small rock rises out of the water. There we spend the night before flying on in the morning."

And the oldest brother continued. "We come here once a year for eleven days to fly over our mother's grave and our father's castle and the people's houses and their fields. Then we must return to the land across the ocean."

"I want to come with you," begged Elisa. "I want to be with you always."

"So be it," said the brothers.

Elisa and her brothers worked all night, weaving a net made from reeds and the thin branches of willow trees.

When the work was done, Elisa fell asleep in the middle of the net. In the morning the brothers turned into swans and, each one holding the net in its beak, they lifted Elisa into the air. The youngest brother flew above her to shade her from the sun's rays. From high above, Elisa looked down on the waves as the swans carried her across the ocean.

They flew all day and into the evening. Elisa saw only waves in the sea. There was no sign of a rock, and the sun was setting. The swans had not been able to fly fast enough because of the weight of their sister and the net.

"It will be my fault if we all perish," cried Elisa in terror to her tired brothers. They made one more effort and flapped their wings with great force. As the sun disappeared below the horizon, Elisa spotted a tiny rock in the dark water below. The swans dived down with such speed that it took Elisa's breath away. The swans had barely touched the rock when they turned into humans.

"Saved!" they cried from their exhausted lungs, and held on to the slippery rock. Elisa and her brothers spent the night clinging to each other and the rock as the wind and the waves beat against them.

In the morning the young men turned into swans again, and they lifted their sister up into the air to carry her to their home in the other land. They flew all day, and the swans got tired from carrying the net and their sister. Still they could not rest. Just as the sun began to set, Elisa looked down to see the shoreline, then the hills and valleys, a castle, a church and a village, people and animals. Everything appeared so tiny from high above. They landed in front of a cave. Not a moment too soon. As they touched the ground, the sun disappeared and the swans turned into young men. The cave was the brothers' home; now it was to be Elisa's home, too.

That evening they did not talk much. They were all very tired from the long flight. Soon the brothers fell asleep. Only Elisa did not sleep. She thought about her brothers and how she could save them from the evil spell. "I'd do anything to help them," she whispered. "I'd even give my life."

That night the beautiful fairy appeared again to Elisa.

"You can save your brothers," said the fairy. "Near this cave and in graveyards, nettles grow. Pick them with your bare hands and stamp on them with your bare feet until the nettles turn into flax. Spin the flax into yarn, and from the yarn weave eleven shirts with long sleeves. When you have finished them all, throw the shirts over the swans. The curse will be broken and your brothers will be free, never to be swans again. But always remember, you must perform this work without speaking one word. If you speak, your work will have been in vain and your brothers will be lost forever. And I must warn you, this work will be very painful, for the nettles will sting your hands and feet like fire."

In the morning, when the swans had flown away, Elisa went outside and began picking the nettles that grew near the cave. Just as the fairy had said, they stung her bare hands like fire until her hands were covered with blisters. When she stamped on the nettles with her bare feet, they hurt as if she had walked on broken glass. Soon her feet were covered with blisters. But finally the nettles turned to flax. Elisa spun the flax into yarn. Now she was ready to make the shirts.

When her brothers returned in the evening, they found Elisa at work. They saw the blisters on her hands and feet.

"What has happened, dear sister?" asked the brothers.

Elisa looked at them with sad eyes, but did not answer.

Somehow the brothers understood that she was trying to help them, and they cried. When their tears fell on Elisa's hands and feet, the blisters disappeared.

Day and night, Elisa worked on the shirts. Soon she had finished five of them. One day, as she sat in front of the cave working on the sixth shirt, she heard the sound of hunters. Quickly she ran inside the cave to hide. But one of the hunters saw Elisa and ran after her.

"Who are you?" said the handsome hunter. "And what are you doing here?"

Elisa did not answer, but looked at him in fear.

The hunter was a young prince. He felt sorry for Elisa. She was so beautiful, and he felt that a cave was a poor place for her to live. Although she struggled against them, the prince and his men took Elisa with them to the castle.

Luckily she was able to take the shirts and the yarn made from the nettles with her.

"Dress this beautiful young lady in fine clothes and take good care of her," said the prince to the ladies-in-waiting.

He was a kind man, but he could not understand why Elisa was not grateful. Every day he went to speak with her. She liked the prince more from day to day. She wanted to tell him how much she appreciated his kindness, and she looked at him with friendly eyes. Every day he loved her more. Her beautiful eyes cheered him up a little, but her silence made him sad.

Elisa finished the sixth shirt, and the seventh, and the eighth. The prince watched her, and more and more he loved her, even though he did not understand her. He could see, though, that with each shirt done, she looked a little less sad. She wanted to tell the prince everything. But most of all she wanted to save her brothers from the evil curse.

When Elisa had finished the tenth shirt, she ran out of yarn. She remembered that the fairy had told her that nettles also grew in graveyards. In the middle of the night, when everyone was asleep, she left the castle and walked to the graveyard. It was a black night

without moon or stars, and dark clouds hung in the sky. On the gravestones sat ugly monsters making horrible noises, as slime dripped from their mouths. They glared at Elisa and shrieked at her. She shivered, but she walked bravely past them to where the nettles grew. Quickly she picked an armful of them and returned to the castle. But someone had been watching. The minister had spied on Elisa and had followed her to the graveyard. The next day he told the prince what he had seen.

By evening Elisa had used up all the nettles that she had picked the night before, and still the last shirt was not done. When she thought everyone was asleep, she again went to the graveyard to pick more nettles. But the prince and the minister followed her secretly. The prince's heart ached as he saw Elisa walk toward the monsters sitting on the gravestones.

"Oh, my God," whispered the prince. "She prefers these hideous monsters to being with me."

"She is a witch," whispered the minister into the prince's ear. Then they fled in horror.

When Elisa returned to the castle with an armful of nettles, two guards arrested her and threw her in jail.

The prince's heart was sad. "How I would like to rescue her," he said to himself. "But the people must judge her."

In the morning, Elisa was brought before the judge and the jury.

"Tell us what you were doing in the graveyard near the monsters," said the judge.

Elisa wanted to scream and tell everything, but she could not and did not. More than anything else, she wanted to finish the shirts. Now how could she? Her eyes begged the prince for understanding and forgiveness.

"You are a witch," said the judge.

"She is a witch," said the jury.

"You are condemned to die like a witch," said the judge.

"She will burn at the stake," said the jury.

The prince heard the judgment with despair, but he was powerless to help Elisa. The people had decided her fate.

Elisa was thrown into jail again until the next morning, when she was to be burned at the stake. She felt that her heart would break. Now what would become of her brothers?

"Here, take your witchcraft," said the prison guard, throwing the nettles and the shirts after her as he slammed the heavy prison door.

Elisa was grateful for the nettles. Now she could finish the last shirt. She worked all night by the light of a tiny candle. "Perhaps, somehow, I can still save my brothers," she thought.

But again she ran out of nettles, and the last shirt was without sleeves.

Early in the morning, before sunrise, the guards put her on a cart, and an old horse pulled her slowly to the stake. Elisa took the shirts with her and held on to them tightly.

"Look at the witch," shouted the people who had come to see her burn.

"Look at her holding on to her witchcraft," laughed someone in the crowd.

Elisa thought her end had come. But just as she was getting ready to leave the cart and walk up the steps to the stake, eleven swans with tiny crowns on their heads flew out of the morning sky. They

flew around her in a circle, then came down on the ground near her. Quickly she threw the shirts over them, and just as quickly they turned into eleven handsome young men. The youngest brother had caught the shirt without sleeves, and instead of two arms he had two wings.

"An angel," whispered the people.

"A miracle," shouted the crowd and fell on their knees.

"Now I can speak," cried Elisa. "I am innocent." And she told the whole story. At the end of the strange tale, the scent of roses filled the air. The wood that had been piled up around the stake had turned into a flowering rosebush.

Overjoyed, the prince stepped forward. He broke off the most beautiful rose and gave it to Elisa.

"Long live the prince!" cheered the people.

"Long live the princess!" said the prince as he took Elisa's hand and led her and her brothers to the castle.

THE WINNERS

One sunny day, a rabbit and a snail met in a field and decided that it would be a good thing to have a race. They asked the fence post to be the judge and a mule to be the timekeeper.

Of course, the rabbit won the race.

"I am first! I won!" shouted the rabbit. "I shall receive the first prize."

A week later, the snail arrived and received the second prize.

"That is an insult," complained the rabbit. "I should have received the second prize as well."

"No," said the fence post, "the snail had to carry her house on her back. That has to be considered. It is a remarkable achievement."

"I should have received the first prize," said a swallow as it flew by. "I am faster than both the rabbit and the snail."

"But," interrupted the fence post excitedly, "you weren't even invited. Besides, you are not a good citizen. Come winter, you fly to another country."

"I should have won the first and the second prize," said the snail. "The rabbit is a coward and he runs out of habit. Always running."

The snail stopped speaking for a day: talking so much had tired her.

Then she continued, "I had to work and concentrate hard to be a runner."

"But . . . but . . ." The fence post tried to say something.

"I should have received the first prize," said the mule. "Being handsome is more important than hard work, speed, or being patriotic."

"You were the timekeeper," spluttered the fence post. "Things are getting out of hand, and, and . . ."

"I think the sunbeam should get the first prize," said a rose growing on the rosebush nearby. "A sunbeam travels faster than anything on earth."

"Wait, wait . . ." screamed the fence post. "Besides, the sunbeam makes me grow," said the rose, ignoring the fence post. It would have been good if the fence post could have screamed or stamped his feet or pulled out his hair. But fence posts are upright and must remain dignified at all times. The whole thing was quite a strain on the poor fence post.

"Who won first prize?" asked a caterpillar who had climbed up the fence post.

That did it! The fence post cracked and fell over.

Now no one will ever know who should have won first prize. Perhaps it doesn't matter.

After all, this is a pretty silly story.

THE BLACKBIRD AND
THE PEACOCKS

One day a young blackbird saw some peacocks. From that moment on, his life was changed.

"Oh, how beautiful they are," he whispered to himself, "and how ugly I am."

Day and night he thought of their beauty. He could neither sleep nor eat.

"If only I could be one of them," moaned the poor blackbird.

He began to follow the peacocks around and when any of them dropped one of its gorgeous feathers, the blackbird would rush to pick it up. Soon he had many of the lovely feathers. He stuck them into his belt.

"Now I am one of them," said the young blackbird as he gazed at his reflection in the mirror. And he flew out to join the peacocks.

He strutted in front of them proudly. But the peacocks had never seen anything so silly as a blackbird with peacock feathers stuck into his belt.

"Hahahaha . . ." they laughed, holding their sides.

A bunch of blackbirds, attracted by all the noise, came out to see what was going on. They, too, had never seen anything so silly as a blackbird dressed up in peacock feathers.

"Hahahaha . . ." they laughed, holding their sides.

The young blackbird ignored them all. "I am a peacock," he insisted.

"The poor creature is touched in the head," said the peacocks.

"Those fine feathers won't fool anyone," agreed the blackbirds. "He is still a blackbird underneath."

THE FOX AND THE CROW

A crow sat high up in a tree with some food in his beak. Below on a park bench sat Mrs. Fox with her son.

"Mama," said the little fox, looking up at the bird, "I wish I had something to eat."

"You *will*," whispered Mrs. Fox into his ear. "Just watch this."

Then, in a slightly louder voice, for the crow to hear, she went on.

"Oh that crow is *so* handsome!"

Upon hearing this the crow ruffled his feathers. He was very pleased.

"Look at his beautiful, shiny coat!"

The crow felt so proud.

"And see his elegant manners!"

If the crow had been a cat he would have purred, that's how happy he felt to hear all these nice things.

"It is said that the crow has a wonderful voice."

"I shall show them how well I can sing," thought the bird and he opened his beak to do so. At that, the food he had been holding fell down to the ground next to the foxes.

"Here, son," said Mrs. Fox and handed him the crow's lunch. "Didn't I tell you that you'd have something good to eat?"

And the crow began to sing.

"Come, son," said Mrs. Fox. "Let's move away from here. I find the crow's song so very irritating."

THE LION AND THE MOUSE

A huge lion sitting on the grass happened to put his foot on a tiny mouse.

"Help, help!" cried the mouse. "Let me out from under here!" And he tickled the lion's paw.

The lion lifted his foot, saw the tiny mouse and held her up to his face.

"Grrrr," growled the lion.

"Please, Mr. Lion," begged the mouse, "don't eat me up."

"Why shouldn't I?" asked the lion. "I am hungry."

"I am so little," said the mouse, "I wouldn't make much of a meal for you."

"You are right," said the lion and he put the mouse down on the ground.

"Thank you," said the mouse as she scurried away. "I'll be glad to help *you* sometime."

"*You* help *me?*" roared the lion, laughing. "That is a joke."

Then the lion stretched out in the shade of a tree and fell asleep. But, just as he began to snore, three wolves sneaked up and threw a heavy rope around him. Before the lion had opened his eyes he was tied securely to the tree. The wolves stole what they could carry of the lion's belongings and ran away, leaving the lion still tied to the tree. No matter how hard the lion pulled, he could not get the rope off. He could not even loosen it.

"Help, help!" howled the lion. When the mouse heard his cry she ran to him.

"Don't worry, Mr. Lion," said the mouse, "I'll help you." And with her sharp teeth she bit through the heavy ropes. In no time she had set the lion free.

"Thank you so much," said the lion, and he set out after the wolves. When he caught up with them, he threw them to the ground and took back all they had stolen from him.

"And now, my dear friend," said the lion as he returned to the mouse, "you have saved my life and my fortune, too. I see that you were not at all too small to do very big deeds!"

"My pleasure," replied the mouse proudly.

THE FROG AND THE OX

Mr. Frog took his family for a stroll. And Mr. Ox took *his* family for a stroll.

As the two families were passing each other, one of the frog children said, "My, look how BIG that ox is!"

"I could be as big as that ox if I wanted to," said Mr. Frog and puffed himself up a little.

"There's no need to puff yourself up like that," said Mrs. Frog, "I like you just the way you are."

"I'm going to be as big as that ox," said Mr. Frog and he puffed himself up some more.

"Papa," said the other frog child, "you were just the right size before."

But Mr. Frog puffed himself up even more, his face turning red.

"Baaaa!" screamed the frog baby, alarmed by the way he looked.

But Mr. Frog puffed himself up still more, his face turning purple.

"Please," shouted the whole frog family. "Don't! We love you the way you are."

But the frog puffed himself up even more than that. The buttons on his coat popped, his pants ripped and his shirt split.

"Stop!" cried Mrs. Frog.

But Mr. Frog gave one more puff and EXPLODED into a thousand pieces.

"Did you hear something go *pop?*" Mr. Ox asked his wife.

"No," replied Mrs. Ox, as they walked on.

71

BIG KLAUS, LITTLE KLAUS

In a village lived two men, both named Klaus. One of them had a large farm and four horses. The other had a small farm and only one horse. The people called the man with the large farm Big Klaus and the man with the small farm Little Klaus.

During the week, Little Klaus worked for Big Klaus. In return, every Sunday, Big Klaus loaned Little Klaus his horses so that he could work his own small field.

Sunday was Little Klaus's happiest day. He loved working his field with five horses.

"Git up, *my* good horses," he shouted proudly when someone passed by.

"They are not *your* horses," said Big Klaus.

"I'm sorry," said Little Klaus.

But the following Sunday, he again shouted, "Git up, my good horses" when someone passed by.

"They are not your horses," scolded Big Klaus. "I'll kill *your* horse if I hear you say that once more."

"I'm sorry," said Little Klaus. "I won't say it again." But the following Sunday, he again shouted, "Git up, my good horses."

At that, Big Klaus, with an axe in his hand, came running from his house and hit Little Klaus's horse so hard on the head that it fell down dead.

Little Klaus cried bitterly. Now he was poorer than ever.

"Pretty soon the people will call me Tiny Klaus," he said weeping. "But perhaps I can sell the horse's skin and make a few pennies," he thought.

He skinned the animal and dried the hide in the wind and sun. When the hide was dry, he put it into a sack and started on his way to the market in town.

74

Little Klaus had never been to town before because he had never
had anything to sell. By evening, he had lost his way, and when darkness set in, he had no idea where he was. After wandering aimlessly
for a long time, he saw light. He walked toward it and came to a
big farm.

He pressed his face against a brightly lit window of the farmhouse,
and looked into the dining room. The farm woman and a gentleman
sat at the table. They were about to have roast beef with dumplings,
served with red wine.

Little Klaus was very hungry. He knocked on the door, hoping
that he would be invited for dinner.

"What do you want?" asked the woman when she saw Little Klaus.

"I have lost my way," answered Little Klaus. "I wonder if I can
stay here until morning."

"My husband is not home," said the woman. "He told me not to
let strangers in." And she slammed the door in his face.

Next to the house stood the barn. Little Klaus climbed up a ladder
into the hayloft to spend the night. But he was thinking about the
roast beef and dumplings. From an open window he looked directly
into the dining room. His mouth began to water and his empty
stomach rumbled loudly.

"Hello up there," bellowed a loud voice from below. "Who is making that rumbling noise?"

It was the woman's husband. He had been away on an errand and had come back much earlier than expected.

"I am a stranger," said Little Klaus, "and I have lost my way. I didn't want to disturb anyone in the house, so I decided to spend the night in your hayloft. I hope you don't mind."

"Come on down," said the farmer. "You are to be my guest and have dinner with us."

"Quick, quick. Hide in the trunk," said the woman to the gentleman upon hearing her husband's loud voice in the yard. The gentleman jumped into an empty trunk and the woman closed the lid. Then she hid the food in the oven and the wine in the cupboard. Little Klaus saw all this before he came down from the hayloft.

As he and the farmer walked into the house, the woman greeted her husband with a false smile and pretended never to have seen Little Klaus. The table was empty and the gentleman was gone.

"Dear wife," said the farmer, "we have a guest. I've invited him to stay for dinner."

She went to the kitchen and returned with a bowl of hot oatmeal. The farmer was hungry and filled his plate and began eating.

But Little Klaus was thinking about the roast beef and dumplings. He had brought along the sack with the hide and had placed it between his feet under the table. He stepped on the hide and it squeaked.

"What was that?" asked the farmer, looking up from his meal.

"It is my wizard," answered Little Klaus. "He tells me that the oatmeal is not good enough for us. He has performed a magic trick and placed roast beef and dumplings in the oven."

76

The farmer got up, went to the oven, and opened the door. Indeed, roast beef and dumplings sat on the shelf.

"You have a fine wizard," said the farmer. "Let me have him. I will pay you five pieces of gold."

"Oh, no, I can't sell him," said Little Klaus. "He is my faithful servant."

Then he stepped on the sack again and the hide squeaked.

"What does your wizard say now?" asked the farmer.

"He tells me that he put a bottle of red wine in the cupboard," said Little Klaus.

The farmer went to the cupboard, reached inside, and found a bottle of red wine.

"I'll pay you ten pieces of gold for your wizard," said the farmer.

But Little Klaus just stepped on the sack again.

"What is it now?" asked the farmer. By this time he was determined to buy that wizard, even if it took all the gold he had.

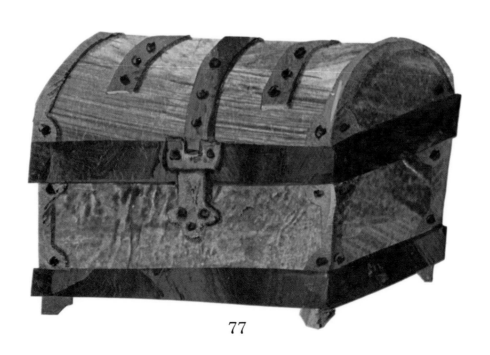

"He tells me that the devil is in there," said Little Klaus, pointing to the trunk. The farmer went to the trunk and opened the lid. By now the gentleman was so frightened that he did indeed look like the devil. The farmer quickly slammed the lid down.

"Go and get a strong rope," he told his wife. He tied the rope around the trunk several times and made a big knot.

"I'll give you fifty pieces of gold for your wizard," said the farmer.

"I can't sell him," said Little Klaus. "He is my faithful servant."

After they had finished their meal, Little Klaus was shown to the guest room, where he slept peacefully until morning. At the breakfast table, over bacon and eggs, the farmer said to Little Klaus, "I'll give you a sack of gold for your wizard."

78

"You have been a good man," said Little Klaus. "I'll let you have the wizard for a sack of gold."

"One more thing," said the farmer as he handed Little Klaus a sack of gold. "Will you take the trunk and dump the devil into the river?"

"Gladly," answered Little Klaus. Together they put the bag of gold and the trunk with the gentleman inside on a wheelbarrow. Then they shook hands, and Little Klaus went on his way.

When he came to the river, he knocked against the trunk.

"Sorry, dear man," said Little Klaus as he began pushing the trunk off the wheelbarrow. "Now I must do what the farmer asked of me."

"Have mercy on me," pleaded the poor gentleman from inside the trunk. "Let me out and I'll give you a sack of gold."

"In that case, I might let you out," said Little Klaus.

He untied the rope and let the gentleman out of the trunk. The gentleman went inside his house, which stood nearby. Soon he returned and handed Little Klaus a sack of gold.

"Not bad," thought Little Klaus. "Two sacks of gold for the skin of one dead horse."

With half a sack of gold, he bought himself five horses. With the other half, he bought a big field near his house. But the sack of gold from the gentleman he kept in his attic.

"Git up, my good horses," shouted Little Klaus proudly as he worked his new field with his five horses.

When Big Klaus saw that, he came running and asked Little Klaus what had happened.

"Oh, I sold the hide from the horse for two sacks of gold," said Little Klaus.

Big Klaus went back to his house, took an axe, and killed his four horses. He skinned and dried the hides and took them to the market.

"Horse hides for sale! Horse hides for sale!" yelled Big Klaus.

"How much?" asked a cobbler who wanted to make shoes from the hide.

"Two sacks of gold for one hide," answered Big Klaus.

"Two sacks of gold!" gasped the cobbler. "You must be crazy. I wouldn't give you more than a piece of silver."

Soon everyone at the market was talking about the crazy man who wanted two sacks of gold for one hide. Several townspeople picked up rocks and threw them at Big Klaus as others screamed, "Get out of here before we beat *your* hide."

Big Klaus ran as fast as he could as rocks came flying after him.

"You'll pay for this, Little Klaus," muttered Big Klaus through his breath as he ran homeward. "I'll kill you!" And as he ran, he tried to think of the best way to get rid of Little Klaus. When he got back to the village, he took a sack, rushed over to Little Klaus, and grabbed him.

"I am going to drown you," he screamed. He threw Little Klaus into the sack and carried him away on his back.

But the sun was hot, the load heavy, and the river a long distance away. When he came to a roadside inn. Big Klaus stopped, put the sack down near the door, and went inside for a glass of beer.

Little Klaus felt uncomfortable. "I am so thirsty. I'd like to have a cool glass of beer myself," he muttered from inside the sack.

"So would I," said a shepherd who happened to pass by. "But I have to keep an eye on my sheep."

"Tell you what," said Little Klaus. "Let me out and I'll watch your sheep while you go into the tavern for a cold glass of beer."

The shepherd liked that. He helped Little Klaus out of the sack and left him with the large herd of sheep. Little Klaus put a heavy rock in the sack and took the sheep to the meadow so that they could graze. After Big Klaus had satisfied his thirst, he picked up the sack with the heavy rock and walked to the river, thinking Little Klaus was still inside.

"Good-bye, Little Klaus," laughed Big Klaus as he pushed the sack into the deep water.

But whom do you think he met on his way home? Yes, Little Klaus with a large herd of snow-white sheep.

"Thank you so much for pushing me into the river," said Little Klaus.

Unable to speak and with big eyes, Big Klaus looked at Little Klaus as if he were a ghost.

"The river goddess at the bottom of the deep river has so many sheep that she doesn't know what to do with them. She was glad that I offered to take some away from her. She has many, many more sheep," said Little Klaus.

Without a word, Big Klaus ran to the river, tied a rope with a heavy stone attached to it around his waist, and jumped into the deep water to see the river goddess and ask her for a herd of snow-white sheep.

Of course, Big Klaus sank to the bottom of the river and was never heard from again.

Little Klaus prospered and lived a happy and long life. And the people called him simply Klaus. After all, there now was only one Klaus in the village.

HANS IN LUCK

Hans had worked seven years with a miller and he felt it was time to go home.

"Seven years have passed, and that is long enough," he said to his master one morning. "I would like to see my mother. Please give me my wages, and I'll be on my way."

"Hans," said the miller, "you have been a good and faithful worker. My wife and I shall miss you, but we wish you the best of luck and a safe trip home."

The miller went to his strongbox and took out Hans's wages. "Here is your pay," he said, and gave Hans a piece of gold the size of his head.

Hans wrapped the gold inside a sack, and threw it over his shoulder. He took his walking stick in his hand, crossed the bridge to the road, and started on his way home.

The road was rough and hilly, and the midmorning sun was hot. Hans began to sweat. The gold seemed very heavy indeed. Just then a horseman came galloping by.

"Ah," said Hans, "a horse is a fine thing. A horseman does not have to carry a heavy load like mine on his back."

"What is in your sack?" asked the horseman.

"It is a piece of gold, and it is quite a lump to carry," said Hans.

"If you like, we will trade," said the horseman. "I will give you the horse and you will give me the gold."

"A good deal," said Hans.

The man helped Hans onto the horse, then made off with the gold as fast as he could. Hans went on his way, feeling lucky to be riding along so easily. But the horse soon understood that Hans was no rider, and Hans was thrown to the ground. A farmer milking his cow in a nearby field stopped the horse and helped Hans to his feet.

Hans was very thirsty. "Dear man," he said to the farmer, "it must be wonderful to have milk whenever you want some. And good fresh butter and cheese, besides. How I would like to have a cow."

"A cow is indeed a very fine thing," replied the farmer, "but a horse can be useful too. If you like, I will trade my cow for your horse."

"A good deal," said Hans. "A horse is not for me. I will never ride that animal again. A cow will suit me better." He took the cow, and the farmer climbed onto the horse and rode away in a great hurry.

Hans felt he was the luckiest man in the world, and he sat down to milk his cow. But milking a cow was something he had never done before and he was clumsy at it. He pushed and pinched and pulled, but the cow would give no milk. Hans tried again, twice as hard. At last the cow became impatient. She raised one of her hind legs and gave Hans a good kick.

Just then it happened that a man was passing by on the road. He had a big fat pig, which he was taking to market.

"Why should the cow kick you?" asked the man.

Hans told of his troubles. "The cow looks poorly," said the man. "Maybe she doesn't give much milk."

"What!" said Hans. "How much better if I had a lovely fat pig like yours. Pork chops and roasts, to say nothing of sausages."

"Well," said the man, "just for you, I'll trade. You take the pig and I'll take the cow."

The exchange was made and Hans set out again. But the pig was stubborn. No matter how much Hans wanted to go one way, the pig wanted to go the other way. Besides, it squealed and screeched and grunted like—well, just like a pig.

Hans was getting discouraged when a woman with a fat goose walked by.

"Eggs for breakfast," Hans thought, "and feathers for a pillow, and a roast for Christmas, all from one bird. Not bad. Perhaps the woman is willing to trade."

The woman knew a good bargain when she saw one and was happy to trade. Hans went on and was close to home when he saw a knife grinder at work. What fun! Sparks were flying through the air, and the grinder's money pouch was full of coins.

"That's a fine goose you have," said the grinder. "Where did you buy it?"

"It was a lucky swap," said Hans, and he told the grinder of all his trades, starting with the lump of gold.

"You've a good head for business," said the grinder. "You should take up my work."

"How can I do that?" said Hans. "I have no grindstone."

"Well," said the grinder, as he picked up a loose cobblestone from the road. "It so happens that I have an extra one. I'll trade it, just for the goose." And so they traded a goose for the old cobblestone.

Hans felt he was the luckiest man in the world. But he had walked a long way and he was very tired and thirsty. The stone grew heavier and heavier every minute. At last he came to a water fountain. He put the stone at the fountain's edge and bent over to take a drink. The stone rolled over and sank deep into the water with a loud *plump*.

Hans laughed. "How lucky I am," he said. "Now I am free, with nothing at all to carry anymore." And he ran home, where his mother saw him coming and rushed to greet him.

"Oh, Hans, how I have missed you," said his mother. "How wonderful it is to have you home again."

She gave him a big, warm hug and led him to the most comfortable chair in the house so that he could sit and rest. Then she bustled around, telling him all the village news while she prepared his favorite supper, a dish of steaming dumplings. Now, more than ever, Hans felt that he was the luckiest young man in the world.

THE SEVEN SWABIANS

There were once seven Swabians who went out to see the world hoping for adventure and the chance to perform brave deeds. For protection they took just one long spear. After days of marching, at last they had their chance. In the middle of a field, they saw a creature sitting with its big eyes wide open and its big ears pricked up. The Swabians had never seen a rabbit before and they thought it was a monster. They lined up along their spear when fear overcame them. Instead of attacking, they cried for mercy:

Only the small Swabian, at the end of the spear's handle, kept pushing—he could not see the rabbit. The others fled in all directions to hide, and the rabbit ran away. When the Swabians thought things safe, they crept out of hiding.

They lined up, grasping their spear, and started marching again. Soon they came to a wide river. There was no bridge across it and there were no boats. A man was working on the other side, and the Swabians called to him, "How can we get across?" He did not understand them, so he called back, "What? What?"

The Swabians thought he was saying, "Wade. Wade." So the leader walked into the water, followed by the other Swabians, each in his place, marching left right, left right, into the river—all except the little one at the end. As usual, he was not paying attention. The six valiant Swabians soon sank to the bottom. When the smallest Swabian saw the leader's hat bobbing along the river, he knew that something was wrong, and returned home to tell this story.

THE WOLF AND THE DOG

A poorly dressed wolf with an empty stomach happened to meet a well-fed and well-dressed dog.

"Ah, hello, Cousin," said the wolf, "How are you?"

"Don't call me 'Cousin,'" answered the dog. "Look at you! In tatters. And begging. It's disgusting! Disgraceful!"

"What a beautiful dress you are wearing," the wolf went on, "and you have such nice plump cheeks. It's clear that you don't know what it is to be hungry."

"I work for my master and he takes good care of me," answered the dog.

"I would like to work for your master, too," said the wolf, "if he'd take as much care of me."

"Well, it just so happens," said the dog, "that my master does need more help."

"What kind of help?"

"We need another watchdog."

"Can I do that?"

"Surely, it's easy. Come along."

As they walked toward the master's house the wolf noticed something around the dog's neck.

"Cousin, what is that thing around your neck?"

"That is a collar."

"What is a collar for?"

"One can attach a chain to it."

"A chain? Whatever for?"

"Watchdogs are often tied on chains outside their masters' houses. Didn't you know that?"

"Thank you, Cousin," said the wolf, turning around. "I know that I'd rather be hungry than chained up like a slave."

And with that the wolf said goodbye and left.

105

THE FOX AND THE CRANE

A stingy fox once invited a crane to his house for dinner. He served a delicious meal but he put it on very flat plates. The poor crane, with her long beak, could not get at the food at all. She turned her neck this way and that way but it didn't help. The food always slipped away from her beak. The fox, pretending not to see the crane's trouble, gobbled up all the food in no time. Of course, the crane was still hungry after the table had been cleared.

"Dear Miss Crane," said the fox as the crane was leaving, "I hope that you have enjoyed your meal. Let's get together soon again."

The crane nodded her head politely, but she did not reply. However, soon afterwards, the crane invited the fox to her house for dinner. She, too, served a delicious meal—but in very tall thin goblets. Of course the fox couldn't get at the food! He tried this way and he tried that way but it didn't help. His food was down at the bottom of the goblet, and no matter how he tried, he couldn't reach it. In the meantime the crane put her long beak down into her tall, thin goblet and easily ate up her meal. This time it was the fox who was still hungry after the table had been cleared.

"Dear Mr. Fox," said the crane as the fox was leaving, "I hope that you have enjoyed your meal. Let's get together soon again."

But the embarrassed fox never again called on the crane.

107

THE WOLF AND THE LAMB

A wolf met a lamb and said to her, "I am hungry. I am going to eat you up."

"My dear wolf," said the lamb, "I understand that perfectly well. That's the way things go. I shall not complain."

"You are a good girl," said the wolf and opened his mouth, showing all his sharp teeth.

"One moment, sir," said the lamb. "As you know, I am entitled to have one last wish."

"That is so, my dear," said the wolf, "and what shall that be?"

"If you would be so kind, I'd like you to play me some music," said the lamb. "I adore music."

The wolf pulled a flute from his pocket and began playing the most beautiful music he could, inspired by the thought of the delectable meal he was about to enjoy.

"You are an artist," whispered the lamb. "Do keep on playing."

Soon the shepherd, hearing unfamiliar music among his lambs, looked to see what was the matter. When he saw the murderous wolf the shepherd took a big stick and hit the wolf over the head.

"Ouch!" yelped the wolf, and he ran into the woods.

THE GRASSHOPPER
AND THE ANTS

All summer long the grasshopper played his fiddle and sang songs. It was a pleasant way to live. Everyone enjoyed his music and he had many friends. There was plenty of food, free for the taking, in the green summer fields. The grasshopper just nibbled a little here and a little there, and then moved on.

The ants, on the other hand, worked hard all summer long collecting food and storing it in their houses.

When it began to get cold, and the snow fell, the grasshopper shivered. His stomach was empty, so he went from ant house to ant house, begging for something to eat.

"While you fiddled last summer," said the ants, "we worked hard putting grain away for the winter time. Now we have just enough for ourselves. Let us alone. Go away."

Poor grasshopper. He was getting hungrier and colder and was beginning to think he would starve to death. Night came and the grasshopper started sadly down the road that led away from the town where everyone had so cruelly refused him food.

Just then he passed the last house. Through the window the grasshopper saw some ants preparing for a holiday feast. Once more he knocked on the door to ask for food. This time, a friendly ant opened it and saw her summertime companion, the grasshopper. Before the grasshopper could say a word she shouted to her family, "Look! Tonight we shall have music!" To the grasshopper she said, "Come in and play and be merry with us."

Together they all celebrated. The ants brought out their most luscious food and the grasshopper played his sweetest music. They danced and they ate and they sang all night long. And everybody was happy.

THE MARSH KING'S DAUGHTER

In Egypt there once lived a happy king. But one day, without warning, great sadness overcame him and stayed with him.

"Melancholy," said his doctors. But they did not know how to cure him.

Friends came to cheer him up, but the king turned away from them. Musicians and dancers performed for him.

"The music hurts my ears, and the dancers offend my eyes," complained the king, and he covered his face with his hands. His cook served him the foods he liked best, but the king left the dishes untouched.

The queen reminded him of the time of their youth, when they were happy together.

"Leave me alone," said the king and walked off.

For days the king sat on his throne not moving, not saying anything, not listening to anyone. He grew thin and pale, but no one knew how to help the poor, sad king. Slowly the people of Egypt laughed less and less, too. They mourned for their king and prayed to their gods to make him happy again.

Now, it happened that the king had a beautiful daughter. Her hair was black as the night, her skin was as white as the feathers of the swan, and her eyes reflected the hues of the sky.

The princess loved her father very much, and she wanted to help him.

One night, when the moon was full, she left the palace. She went to the Sphinx in the desert.

"Wise one," said the princess, "you must help my father."

The Sphinx, half man, half lion, and made of stone, remained silent. But his eyes told the princess to go to the pyramid.

There she found a secret entrance. A dark tunnel led to the middle of the pyramid. At the end of the tunnel, a strange light flickered, beckoning her to come closer. The princess carefully made her way toward it until she reached a spot where a single ray of moonlight fell through a crack in the roof of the cave onto the dead body of the Great King. Like the other kings of Egypt who had died, he had been wrapped as a mummy in white linen, and a golden mask had been put over his face. There he lay, a mummy, amid all his treasures.

"I have been waiting for you," said the mummy without moving his lips. "I am your great-great-great-great-grandfather. Listen, my child. I know why you have come. Go to the land of the Vikings in the north. There you will find a wild marsh. In the middle is a lake. On its water grows an amber flower. Bring the flower to your father, the king of Egypt."

"How shall I get there?" asked the princess.

"Put a swan skin over your body. When the storks fly north in the springtime, fly with them. They know the way," answered the mummy.

The tiny ray of moonlight had moved away and it was dark and quiet again in the burial chamber of the Great King. Groping her way along the stone wall, the princess found her way out of the pyramid and went back to the palace.

In the morning she asked one of her father's hunters to kill a swan and bring its skin to her. Soon it was springtime. The storks, who had built a nest on the tower of the palace, grew restless, and the princess knew that the time had come.

She threw the swan skin over herself. Immediately she became a swan. She spread her wings, lifted herself into the air, and flew northward with the storks. It was a long flight over the sea, islands, mountains, and valleys, over big cities with beautiful cathedrals, and over wheat fields with peasants' huts.

After many days the princess arrived in the land of the Vikings. Below her she saw a wild marsh. In the middle of the marsh was a dark lake. In it grew an amber flower, just as the dead king had said. Its strange beauty seemed to pull the princess out of the sky. She landed at the edge of the water, took off the swan skin, and hid it in the tall reeds. A dead tree had fallen, forming a bridge from the edge of the lake to the flower in the water. Balancing herself carefully, the princess walked on the dead tree toward the flower.

Suddenly the tree moved. The princess fell into the lake. She cried for help as a gnarled branch pulled her slowly under the water. Nobody heard her. Greenish bubbles rose one by one to the surface. The flower swayed lightly for a brief moment, then the lake was as smooth and silky as if nothing had happened. Not a trace of the princess could be seen. Down, down, down she went.

What she had thought was a dead tree was really the marsh king

himself, who had tricked the princess of Egypt. He had put his arm around her and had pulled her down into his dark, slimy kingdom.

Summer went by. Autumn came, and the storks went back to Egypt in the south. The amber flower withered and sank to the bottom of the lake. Winter came, and the cold winds blew snow over the land of the Vikings.

At last, spring returned, and with it came the storks. One stork flew over the wild marsh and saw a mysterious flower in the lake. It grew from a large, round green leaf. He flew closer and saw, sitting

on the leaf, a beautiful baby girl with black hair, white skin, and eyes that reflected the hues of the sky.

It happened that the stork and his family had their nest on top of the Viking castle. Many times the stork had heard the Viking queen say to the Viking king, "It is so sad that we are without a child. Oh, how I wish that we would have one."

Now, the Viking king and his rough warriors had sailed across the North Sea to burn and plunder the kingdoms on the far shores. Whenever the king was away, the queen felt lonesome and wished for a child more than ever.

"Well," said the stork to himself, "I'll take this beautiful baby girl to the queen. She has truly waited long enough."

The Viking queen was overjoyed to have her long-yearned-for child. She hugged and kissed the baby, the most precious gift she could have asked for. But the baby kicked and screamed and scratched like a wild cat. The queen did not mind. After all, her wish had come true.

Finally, toward evening, the child fell asleep, and the queen put her to bed, drawing the curtain to protect the tiny thing from the cold.

In the middle of the night the queen woke up and thought of her child. Full of love, she went to look at the baby. She drew the curtain aside—but what was this? There was no baby, but in the middle of the bed sat an ugly frog.

The queen wanted to scream and run, but the frog croaked pitifully as if to say, "Hold me." The queen held the ugly frog in her hands and sat down, looking at the miserable creature. It had such sad eyes and made such whimpering sounds that the queen felt sorry for it. She looked at the ugly frog for a long time, not knowing what to do. After a while she fell asleep sitting in the chair and holding the frog in her lap.

In the morning the sun's rays came through the window and woke the queen. In her lap sat a tiny, beautiful baby girl who kicked and screamed and scratched like a wild cat the moment the queen opened her eyes.

"I must have had a bad dream," said the queen to herself.

The following night she again went to see the child, but again the ugly frog sat in the bed. It looked at her sadly, saying, "Croak, croak" in a soft, woeful voice.

Now the queen knew that her child was bewitched and she decided to keep it a secret.

A few days later, the Viking king and his warriors returned with slaves and gold. Usually at this time they feasted for seven days and nights. When the king found that his queen had had a child while he was gone, he ordered everyone to celebrate for fourteen days and nights, such was his joy. He named his daughter Helga.

Time passed, and the wild, beautiful child grew into a cruel, beautiful, and ferocious woman. The little ugly frog grew into a big ugly frog. Helga grew nastier and more hateful as the frog frew more tender and affectionate. Sometimes the queen thought sadly that she loved the frog more than she did Helga.

The king liked his wild daughter. He was a warrior, and he admired her rough manner.

"She will become a great warrior," he said proudly to anyone who would listen. Soon he went off again to plunder other countries.

When the Vikings returned, they brought slaves and gold. One of the slaves was handsome and gentle. He did not complain about the ropes that bound his hands and feet. He forgave his tormentors for their cruelty as they pulled him by his soft blond beard. And he spoke to them of love and peace. He did not beg for food or ask for water. He was calm and quiet, as if these rough people could do him no harm.

Helga hit him with a horsewhip, hurled insults at him, and spat in his face. He looked at her calmly. "One day, not far from now, you, too, will understand the meaning of love and peace," he told her quietly.

She was unable to gaze at his kind face. But for just one brief moment she looked into his loving eyes, and she felt something stir in her heart. A voice within herself said, "Trust him." "Never," said another voice.

"Pierce his feet and pull the rope through them," demanded Helga. "Tie him to a wild bull and have him dragged across the sharp rocks on the beach."

Her cruelty frightened even the king, and he ordered that the gentle slave be taken to the cellar and left alone.

"You have brought me much sorrow," said the queen to the ugly frog that night. "You have made me suffer. Your heart is as black as the deep in the wild marsh. My soul aches. But I love you. Oh, what will become of us all?"

The ugly frog listened and moaned from the depth of her sad heart.

When the queen had gone to bed and fallen asleep, the frog waddled on her webbed feet to the door, unlocked it, and went to the gentle slave in the cellar. The frog took a knife and cut the ropes by which the slave was tied to a heavy beam. Then the frog motioned him to follow. They went to the royal stables, and the frog pointed to a beautiful black stallion—Helga's prize horse. The slave and the frog jumped on the horse and escaped into the night, away from the Viking castle.

They rode all night through the forest, over meadows, past waterfalls.

In the morning, when the sun rose, the ugly frog turned into Helga, the cruel, wild woman. Her beauty almost blinded the gentle slave.

She pulled a knife from her belt.

"Now I shall kill you, you fool," screamed Helga and raised her knife to slash the young man.

"Do not hate me. Look into my eyes; there you will find the truth," he said. His words took all the power of her hatred from her breast. Her hand dropped the deadly knife to the ground, where it broke into many pieces. A strange sense of peace and warmth came over her. She no longer resisted his gaze. His eyes were like two mirrors. In one she saw her mother, the princess of Egypt, and the marsh king who held her against her will. In the other, Helga saw her grandfather, the king of Egypt, holding his hand out for an amber flower.

"You have broken the spell," whispered Helga. She reached for his hands, to hold them.

"Now that you have found me, I must leave. But know that I will come back," said the handsome slave. They embraced for one brief moment. Then he disappeared into the rays of the morning sun.

"There is much to be done," said Helga and jumped onto the black stallion and galloped—no, flew, on golden wings, across the land.

"Hooo," whispered Helga into the horse's ear as she saw the wild marsh below. They drifted slowly down to the edge of the dark lake. The water was smooth and silky. Helga saw herself reflected on its surface as if it were a mirror.

"My child," cried the reflection. She reached out and put her arms around her daughter.

Then Helga understood that this was not a reflection in the water. It was her mother, the princess of Egypt.

"All these years have been a nightmare. I could see you grow up and I knew of your unhappiness, but I could not help you. I wanted to speak to you. I wanted to hold you and tell you that your mother loved you, but I have been held down a prisoner in eternal darkness," said the princess. "The marsh king took pity on me and finally released me. I could never be his."

At that moment, the marsh king's webbed hand reached out of the murky water. In his palm lay an amber flower. He gave it to the princess.

The princess found the swan skin in the tall reeds where she had hidden it many years before. She put it over her body and rose into the autumn air, followed by Helga on her golden-winged black stallion. The storks, too, flapped their wings. It was time to fly south, back to Egypt.

The marsh king looked for one brief moment at his beautiful daughter before he sank into his wet kingdom.

"Come, my child," said the princess. "We must go home to Egypt."

"Yes, my mother," said Helga. She jumped onto the golden-winged stallion and with her mother rose into the autumn air. But Helga remembered the Viking queen.

The Viking queen had indeed missed her Helga. When it was discovered that the gentle slave had escaped also, she knew that Helga had freed him.

Every night for years she had left her bed to look at the ugly frog behind the curtain while her husband, the king, snored. The frog had disappeared along with Helga, but the queen still arose. Now she looked out the window.

"What does it all mean?" She spoke softly as if the moon and the stars could answer her. At that moment, Helga flew down from the dark sky.

"Kind foster mother, you have been so good to me, and I will always remember you," said Helga. "Now I must leave you forever. I have caused you much pain. I know that I need not ask your forgiveness, because you always knew that I had no power over my evil self. The gentle slave has lifted the spell and I love him."

The two women held each other closely and Helga continued, "Your king and his warriors will come to understand the message of the slave—the message of peace and love. They will stop plundering and taking slaves and will become farmers and artisans."

The two looked at each other one more time before Helga joined her true mother, the princess of Egypt, in the air, where she had been waiting. Now they and the storks began their long journey home.

They flew for many days until at last they saw the Sphinx, the Great Pyramid, and the Nile River. They were home.

The king of Egypt was much older now, but he was still very ill and sad. Even the return of his long-lost daughter did not cheer the pale, feeble old man.

Then the princess held out the amber flower to her father—the gift of happiness for which he had waited so long.

The king's eyes began to sparkle. He smiled. He chuckled, and finally laughed out loud. His pale cheeks turned pink.

"Thank you, my daughter, thank you," said the king through tears of joy, as he hugged both the princess and Helga.

Soon the people of Egypt heard that their king was happy again. And they, too, laughed again and thanked their gods for listening to their prayers.

In the days that followed, Helga often thought about her good foster mother and the gentle slave. Spring came, and Helga engraved a golden ring with the words "Love, Helga" and asked the stork who had a nest on top of the palace to take the ring to the Viking queen.

But would she ever see her gentle slave again? Had he not promised to come back? Since the day he had disappeared, she could not forget his mirror-like eyes.

As she waved the stork good-bye, a caravan of camels, led by one man, moved slowly from the desert toward the palace. The caravan stopped at the gate, and the man asked for Helga. His robe hid his body, and his turban covered most of his face. Only his eyes looked gently, softly at Helga.

"Will you come with me?" asked the man.

"Yes," said Helga quietly.

The gentle slave had come to take her with him to his land across the desert.

THE TRAVELING COMPANION

Johann was sad. His father was very ill and Johann knew that he was going to die.

"Don't be unhappy," said his father. "I have had a good life. I cannot complain. And you have been a fine boy. Now I shall join your mother," said the father, and he closed his eyes as his heart stopped.

Johann's mother had died a long time ago. Johann was so lonely that he wept into the night until finally he fell asleep.

When he woke up in the morning, he was still holding on to his father. He took his hand out of his father's and discovered a silver coin in his palm.

Johann called the pastor and had his father buried. He put flowers on the grave and stood there for a long time. Then he packed a few things, put the silver coin into his pocket, and marched away from his village into the world.

All day he walked through meadows, woods, and towns. In the evening he chose a deserted barn as his night quarters. He put down his pack, took off his shoes, and fell asleep.

Suddenly he saw his mother pointing at a beautiful princess with a golden crown on her head.

"She will be your bride," said his mother, and the princess smiled at him.

Johann opened his eyes, but only the moon smiled at him through an opening in the roof of the barn. The dream kept him awake. Since he could not sleep, he took his pack, put on his shoes, and stepped into the night. Before long, he passed a churchyard. In the middle of it was an open coffin, and nearby stood two wicked-looking men. Johann could tell that they were up to no good.

"Hey, what are you doing?" he asked as he walked up to them.

"This man owes us money," said one of the men, pointing to a corpse in the coffin, "but he decided to cheat us out of it by dying. Now we'll take his clothing and whatever else we can find on him and sell them. We'll teach him to cheat us."

"Here, take this," said Johann, and he handed his silver coin to the two wicked men. "Will this pay his debt?"

"That'll do," said one of them, and grabbed the coin.

"What a fool," said the other as they fled into the night.

Johann stayed all night near the coffin, to make certain that the two men did not return. In the morning he saw to it that the dead man got a decent burial. Only then did he leave.

Soon he felt hungry, but he had nothing to eat and no money to buy food.

"Hello there," said someone from behind him. "Where to?"

"Oh, I'm going to see the world," said Johann, turning around to see a tall and friendly man.

"Mind if I join you?" asked the man.

"Not at all," said Johann. "I'd be glad to have a traveling companion."

They shook hands and walked on together. They talked and laughed and found they liked each other.

"I am hungry," said the traveling companion after a while. "How about something to eat?"

He sat down on the grass and opened his pack. Out came the most wonderful things to eat: sausage, bread, apples, cheese, and much more.

"Sit down, my friend," said the traveling companion. "What's mine is also yours."

Johann, of course, didn't need to be told twice.

"How can I repay you?" asked Johann.

"You have already paid, by accepting me as your traveling companion," the man answered.

At that moment an old woman walked by. On her head she carried a large basket filled with sticks of firewood. As she looked at the two men, to return their "good day," she tripped and fell and broke her leg.

"Oh, oh, aw, aw," cried the poor woman, in pain.

The traveling companion pulled a small green bottle from his pocket. He put one drop of it on her leg, and the old woman stood up as if nothing had happened. She gathered the sticks into the basket. When she had finished, she said, "You have healed my broken leg. What can I do for you?"

"Let me have three of the strongest sticks," answered the traveling companion.

"Please, help yourself," said the woman.

The man picked the three strongest sticks and put them into his pack.

The two friends walked on, talking and laughing, gladder than ever that they had found each other. In the evening they came to a town and went to an inn where they could stay overnight.

The dining room at the inn was filled with merry travelers. They ate and drank and sang and told stories. Johann sat with his mouth open, listening to strange tales from all corners of the world.

Suddenly a loud scream came from the kitchen. The cook had wanted to cut off a rooster's neck, but his sharp knife had slipped, and he had cut off one of his own fingers instead.

The traveling companion looked at the damage, then reached for the little green bottle in his pocket. He put two drops from it on the cook's hand. And before you could say "gee whiz," the cook had five perfect fingers on his hand.

"You have been good to me," said the cook. "What can I do for you?"

"Let me have the sharp knife," said the traveling companion.

"Here, take it," said the grateful cook, and the traveling companion put it into his pack.

The next day, Johann and his friend marched on. They walked up a mountain. When they reached the top, an eagle dropped from the sky and fell dead in front of them.

The traveling companion took the sharp knife, cut off both the eagle's wings, and, without saying a word, put them into his pack.

In the evening they came to a large city. As they walked past the guard and through the gates, a carriage, drawn by four black stal-

lions, passed them. Through the window of the carriage, Johann saw a beautiful young woman with a golden crown on her head. She was the very same woman he had seen in his dream, and who his mother had said would become his bride.

"Tell me," said Johann excitedly to the guard, "who is she?" He pointed toward the disappearing carriage.

"She is the king's daughter," said the guard.

"She is beautiful," said Johann to himself, but the guard heard him.

"Young man," he said, "you'd do yourself a favor to forget her. She may be beautiful, but she is a witch."

"What do you mean?" asked Johann.

"She has announced that anyone can ask to marry her," said the guard, "be it prince, merchant, soldier, peasant, or pauper. It doesn't matter to her as long as her suitor can answer any three questions she asks him. So far, no one has been able to guess right, and she has had their heads chopped off."

The traveling companion, who had listened, said to Johann, "Forget her. She is trouble."

The two found an inn to stay for the night. But Johann could not sleep. He could think only of the beautiful princess.

In the morning he went to the castle and knocked on the big iron gate. The king himself opened the heavy door and asked, "What do you want?"

"I want to marry the princess," answered Johann.

"Oh, my dear fellow," sighed the king. "You don't know what you are talking about. My daughter is bewitched. You must leave. You are too young to die. You see, I have promised her that she could have any man that she wanted and I would not interfere. Never did I dream that she would chop off her suitors' heads if they couldn't guess the answers to her questions."

"I love her," said Johann, as if he hadn't heard a word the king said.

"Come with me and see for yourself," said the king, and he led Johann by his sleeve to a window. Through the window the king pointed to the princess's garden. What a sight! From the trees hung dozens of skeletons, rattling in the wind. And instead of rows of flowers, there were rows of skulls on the ground.

"Those were once young men like you, who wanted to marry her," said the king.

"She is so beautiful," mumbled Johann.

"You must be crazy," said the king. "I wish you would change your mind, but since you won't, I'll introduce you to the princess. Here she comes."

Johann's face turned red. The princess was even more beautiful than in the dream. She was also very friendly and offered him tea and cookies.

"Well, my dear Johann, you must visit me tomorrow," said the princess, "and I'll ask you the first of three questions." With a sweet smile, she added, "If you cannot answer my question, I'll have your head chopped off."

Back at the inn, the traveling companion said to Johann, "Let's celebrate. Tonight may be your last." And he ordered a bottle of wine.

The traveling companion took the green bottle from his pocket and put a drop from it into Johann's wine. And they lifted their

glasses and said, "Cheers!" Soon the drop from the green bottle put Johann to sleep. He snored so loudly that the whole room shook.

Shortly before midnight, the traveling companion took the eagle's wings from his pack and fastened them with straps onto his shoulders. He also took one of the sticks that the woman who had broken her leg had given to him.

Then, using the eagle's wings, he flew toward the castle and landed on the roof above the princess's room. At midnight her window opened and out she flew. The traveling companion took the green bottle from his pocket and rubbed three drops from it behind his ear. At once he became invisible. He followed the princess into the black night and beat her with the stick. She thought it was a hailstorm. "Oh, how it hails. Oh, how it hails," she screamed.

She flew quickly to the mountain. When she knocked three times against it, the mountain opened. The princess, followed by the invisible traveling companion, walked into a dark cave. In the middle of it stood a throne made from human bones. On the throne sat a wizard.

"Hee, hee, hee, here comes my bride," croaked the wizard.

The princess bowed low and kissed the wizard.

"Tomorrow a new suitor will ask me to marry him," said the princess. "What question shall I ask him?"

"Ask him to guess your thought," said the wizard. "Choose something so simple he'll never think of it. How about your shoe?"

The invisible companion heard every word. The princess curtsied, and the wizard opened the mountain.

As the princess flew back to the castle, the traveling companion again beat her with the stick.

"Oh, how it hails. Oh, how it hails," she cried.

She came to the castle and flew through the window and into her room. The traveling companion flew back to his own room, took off the wings, went to bed, and fell asleep. In the morning the magic had worn off. He was visible again.

"I had a strange dream about the princess and her shoe," he told Johann.

"That might be the answer to her question," Johann said cheerfully. "Who knows?" And he went off to the castle.

The princess smiled, but the king looked sad.

"Good morning, my friend," said the princess to Johann. "What am I thinking about?"

"Your shoe," said Johann without hesitation.

The princess turned white and whispered, "Yes."

The king jumped up and down with joy. In the evening, Johann and the traveling companion celebrated again.

The traveling companion again put a drop from the little green bottle into Johann's wine, and Johann fell asleep and snored. The traveling companion strapped on the wings, took two sticks with him, and made himself invisible. He followed behind the princess to the mountain, but this time he beat her with two sticks.

"Oh, how it hails. Oh, how it hails," cried the princess, wincing as stroke after stroke beat down on her.

"The suitor guessed right," said the princess to the wizard after she had kissed him.

"Ah, we have to make it a little more difficult," hissed the wizard. "Think about your *gloves*."

In the morning the traveling companion told Johann that he had dreamed about the princess and her gloves, and Johann guessed right for the second time. The princess fainted. But the king jumped up and down with joy.

The third night, the traveling companion followed the princess again. This time he took three sticks and the sharp knife with him.

"Oh, how it hails. Oh, how it hails," screamed the princess as the traveling companion beat her without mercy with the three sticks.

She told the wizard that Johann had guessed right again.

"There must be a spy here," said the wizard. "Let's not talk in here."

The wizard flew with the princess back to the castle. The traveling companion beat them both terribly with the three sticks, and they both cried, "Oh, how it hails. Oh, how it hails."

"Think of my head," whispered the wizard before the princess disappeared through the window into her room. But the traveling companion heard it all. He followed the wizard back to the mountain, beating him with all his might. Just as the wizard was about to disappear into the cave, the traveling companion took the sharp knife and cut off the wizard's head. He wrapped it in his handkerchief, returned to his room, and fell asleep.

In the morning, Johann got ready to go and see the princess for the third time.

"Today she will be mine," whistled Johann, combing his hair in front of the mirror.

"Here," said the traveling companion, "take this with you." He gave Johann the handkerchief. "Don't open it until the princess asks you what she is thinking about."

"What am I thinking about?" asked the princess. She looked more beautiful than ever. The king looked sadder than ever.

Johann unfolded the handkerchief, and out fell the wizard's head.

"You shall be my husband," said the princess, barely breathing. Then she turned ashen white and fainted away.

The king jumped up and down with joy and shouted to the people who had gathered outside his castle. "Tonight is the wedding. Have the church bells ring. We'll have a party."

The king invited the whole kingdom to the wedding celebration. There were dancing and fireworks, wine and cake, roasted pigs and delicious chocolate pudding, and much more.

Things were not as happy as they seemed, though. Johann did not know it, but the princess was still bewitched and she did not love him at all.

"Here, take this," said the traveling companion after the celebration. He gave Johann the little green bottle. "Before you and the princess go to bed, sprinkle four, then five, then six drops on her."

When the princess had put on her nightgown and was about to go to bed, Johann sprinkled four drops on her. Thunder and lightning shook the castle as if the world had come to an end, and the princess turned into an eagle.

Now Johann sprinkled five drops on the eagle. Again there was thunder and lightning, and screams as if all the demons had been let loose. And the eagle turned into the wizard.

Now Johann sprinkled six drops on the wizard. The moon and stars appeared in the lovely night sky, and not a sound could be heard. The wizard turned into the princess, more beautiful than ever. She held Johann's hand and kissed his face.

"Thank you, my dear Johann," she said with tears of joy in her eyes. "You have broken the evil spell that hung over me."

In the morning the traveling companion came to Johann and the princess to bless them and to say good-bye.

145

"We want you to stay," said Johann and the princess, putting their arms around him. "You are our friend and we want to repay you for all that you have done for us."

"No, my time is up," said the traveling companion. "Johann, you have more than repaid me. Do you remember the two wicked men who tried to rob the dead man in his coffin?" The traveling companion touched Johann on his shoulder, saying, "I am the dead man."

Johann and the princess reached out for the traveling companion, but he had disappeared as if he had never existed.

Johann and the princess had many, many children, and the old king enjoyed being a grandfather more than ruling his people.

"Johann," he said one day, "you be the king and let me be the baby-sitter."

And that is how Johann became king.

He ruled wisely and happily and was loved by everyone.

THE EVIL KING

Once there lived a king, and everybody called him the Evil King. The Evil King was the only one who did not know that. In fact, he liked to think of himself as the Good King.

His ministers, secretaries, generals, and knights all called him the Good King to his face. But behind his back they called him the Evil King. Why was he so evil?

He had decided to conquer the whole world. His army attacked town after town, country after country. He did not spare his enemies. He killed them or made them into his slaves. He stole gold and jewels, burned houses to the ground, destroyed animals and food supplies. He put chains around the necks of the vanquished kings. He made them crawl on their hands and knees, and threw bones to them for food.

The more his opponents suffered, the more the Evil King laughed his evil laugh. It was a great joy to him to see others cry in despair.

One day, after many tears and much bloodshed everywhere, the Evil King had conquered the whole world. He ordered his craftsmen to melt down all the stolen gold and make statues of himself. In the middle of every town, a statue of the Evil King, with a plaque saying "The Good King," was erected.

"Now what?" said the Evil King to himself, looking out the window into the sky. "Ah!" he shouted. "I shall conquer the heavens!"

He ordered his slaves to build an airship with a hundred cannons on board. At each of the Evil King's commands, each cannon could fire a dozen cannonballs. When the airship was finished, a thousand strong eagles were hitched to it. Then the Evil King and his army went aboard.

"Fly," ordered the Evil King, and the eagles rose and pulled the mighty airship into the sky.

The Evil King sat on a golden throne, and when he thought that he was close enough to the sun, he shouted. "Fire! Fire! Fire!" Cannonball after cannonball flew with great noise and speed toward the sun.

But the sun's hot rays melted the cannonballs, and the molten metal fell on the eagles and the airship. The great airship shuddered. The eagles stopped flying. The cannons stopped firing. The warriors screamed in panic. The king held on to his golden throne as the airship fell and crashed into the countryside. Everyone perished except the king. He landed in a tree whose branches and leaves held him and saved him.

"I shall conquer the universe!" shouted the Evil King as he climbed from the tree. "I am the mightiest ruler ever. Nothing will stop me."

He ordered his slaves to build an even mightier airship and to make cannonballs that he hoped could not be melted by the sun. For seven years the slaves worked day and night. The new airship had a thousand cannons on board. Each one could fire a hundred cannonballs at each command by the Evil King. A hundred thousand strong eagles were hitched to the airship. Then the king and his army went aboard.

People from all over the kingdom had been ordered to come and see the new and mightier airship rise into the sky. Before take-off, the king spoke.

"I shall conquer the universe," shouted the king, pounding his fist on the golden throne. "Nobody can stop me. I am the greatest. I shall destroy the sun and enslave the moon and burn the whole universe."

Just then, a tiny mosquito buzzed into the Evil King's ear and stung him. The pain burned like liquid fire, and the king jumped up and down. He slapped his ear with his hand. He knocked his head against a cannon. But the pain would not go away.

Crazy with desperation, the Evil King tore off his clothes and stood on his head, hoping that the little insect would fall out. The naked king shrieked and shouted and wiggled his legs. But the pain would not go away. Have you ever seen a naked king stand on his head crying and kicking his legs into the air?

151

Well, the people and the soldiers did. They giggled at first, and then broke out laughing. Soon the whole kingdom shook with laughter. "Hahahahahahahahahah," they jeered, slapping their bellies and stamping their feet.

Now if there is one thing an Evil King cannot stand, it is his people laughing at him. When the pain in his ear went away, the Evil King looked up and saw his people laughing at him. He grabbed the coat of the nearest soldier, covered himself, and ran and ran and ran—never to be seen again.

That, my friends, was the end of the Evil King who conquered the world and who was conquered by a tiny mosquito.

It is also the end of my storybook.

ABOUT THE AUTHORS

It is hard to imagine our childhood literature without the wise and witty fables of Aesop. Of his life we have only the scantiest information. It is believed that he was a Greek slave, living in the 6th century B.C., whose nimble wit so often saved his master from trouble that he was finally allowed to earn his freedom. His tales have been retold in many languages, yet through all their transformations they have retained the mark of an original genius. They were translated into English and published by William Caxton in 1484.

The brothers Grimm, Wilhelm (1789–1859) and Jakob (1785–1863), were linguists and scholars who worked harmoniously as a team throughout their lives. After the classicism and restraints of the 18th century there had come a desire not only for beauty but also for strangeness and mystery, and out of this was born the Romantic movement in literature. The folk and fairy stories the Grimms collected from the common people near their home in Hesse, Germany, were published in 1812–1824. Their immediate popularity may have surprised the serious brothers, but with their elves, dwarves and talking animals of the forest, their peasants and princesses, they fitted the Romantic mode perfectly. They were translated and published in England in 1823–1826, with illustrations by George Cruikshank, where they were read and enjoyed by adults and children alike.

Hans Christian Andersen was born in 1805 in the town of Odense, Denmark. His family was poor—his father was a cobbler and his mother took in laundry. Nevertheless, Andersen's childhood was happy and always full of golden memories for him. Though he was frustrated in his desire to be an actor and playwright, his first book of travel stories was well-received and his gifts as a storyteller were appreciated. He lived, however, at the edge of poverty as a young man, and never lost his sympathy for the struggles of the poor. In 1839 his first little book of tales for children appeared, soon to be followed by another, and then he began to produce a new collection each year. At first, as he explains in his autobiography, he retold old stories in his own way as he remembered hearing them in his youth. Later he came to rely more on his own inventiveness.

Always known as a witty conversationalist and a wonderful storyteller, he finally achieved some financial success. On his visits to Germany, he became friendly with the brothers Grimm, whom he greatly admired. Andersen's tales, however, differ from those of the Grimms. Andersen's stories are more strongly rooted in the familiar. The furniture and toys of the nursery, the animals and creatures of the barnyard are his most frequent characters —they think and talk as children think and talk. As a storyteller, however, he wrote for a wide audience and his stories, while they appeal directly to children, almost always contain a deeper message for adults.

ABOUT THE ARTIST

Eric Carle's many beloved books for children are known and loved around the world. Born in Syracuse, New York, in 1929, he received his education at the Akademie den bildenden Künste in Stuttgart, Germany. Returning to the United States, he worked as a graphic artist and designer and then became the art director of a large advertising agency, before deciding to devote himself entirely to creating picture books for children. He now lives in Massachusetts. His distinctive illustrations, executed in intricately colored and layered collages, have instant appeal for young readers. His original stories, too, while seemingly simple, touch children's deepest feelings. All of them, though couched in humor and fantasy, contain kernels of wisdom that linger in the mind like the fables of Aesop or some of the stories of Andersen and the brothers Grimm.

Folk tales have always been reinterpreted and amplified in their passage from mouth to mouth and culture to culture. In his lively retellings of the classic stories in this volume, Eric Carle has followed the long oral tradition, retaining the essentials of the tales, but making such alterations as he felt were called for. In general, he has kept to the plots of the stories faithfully, but in some he has eliminated long descriptive passages that he felt were obstacles to young people just beginning to have some mastery of reading. The stories he has selected are those he remembers enjoying when he was himself a child. His versions are based partly on childhood memory and partly on consultation both with the original texts and with those of such folklorists as Andrew Lang, Joseph Jacobs and Ludwig Bechstein. Here is everything that is satisfying in the old folklore and legends: brave deeds, familiar animals, hints of sparse but adventurous peasant living, glimpses of royal splendor. As both storyteller and illustrator, Eric Carle has achieved a compelling unity of effect that captures the homely wisdom, fantasy and humor of these childhood favorites.

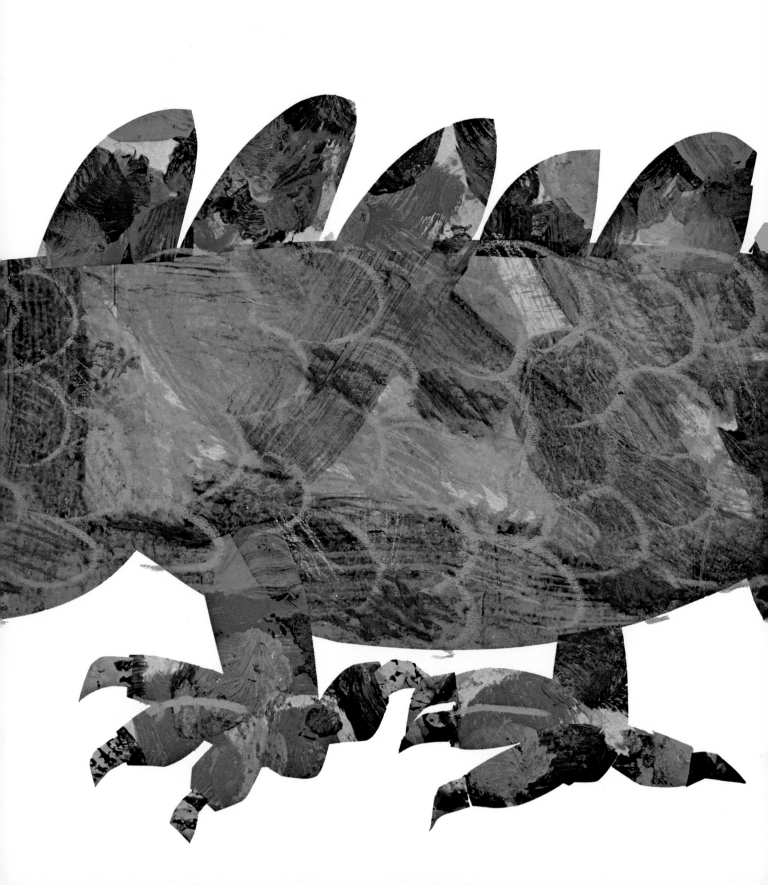